BALM IN GILEAD
Broken Saints Act 2

Sherman Cox

DISCARDED

Copyright© 2016 Sherman Cox

All Rights Reserved.

No part of this book may be used or reproduced by any means, graphic, electronic, or mechanical, including photocopying, recording, taping or by any information storage retrieval system without the written permission of the publisher except in the case of brief quotations embodied in critical articles and reviews.

All characters, names, descriptions, and traits are products of the author's imagination. Similarities of actual people – living or dead are purely coincidental.

Version 1.0

Connect with Sherman Cox
Twitter: @shermancox
Website: www.shermancox.com
Blog: www.shermancox.com/blog
Facebook: https://www.facebook.com/shermancox

CHAPTER 1

Earl Ellington slowly walked into the pastor's study. A smile graced his face.

He hadn't planned on any of it happening. He didn't know he would be where he is. However, now he was sitting in the driver's seat as the pastor, well interim pastor, of Arise Community Worship Center.

The room he had so many times sat in while Pastor Harold told him about the ministry and what it was about almost celebrated with him.

What would his mother think? She never helped him, but now he was somebody. So he thought.

The smile on his face threatened to become permanent as he already began making plans for the future of the church.

Those plans were interrupted as his cell phone buzzed.

He reached in his pocket and pulled it out. He glanced at the caller ID.

It was Reverend Dwayne Dexter, the womanizing associate pastor that wanted to be pastor probably more than Earl did.

Earl laughed.

He probably wants me to help him become the permanent senior pastor, Earl thought.

Earl pressed the ignore button on the call.

It buzzed again almost immediately.

The caller ID said Carolyn Harold.

Yeah, she wants to talk now. Never has time, but now she wants to talk, Earl thought.

He loved her, he really did, but he didn't really want to talk to her now., especially in light of the fact that he was pastor and her brother, Trey, was on the outside looking in.

He ignored the call.

The phone rang again. This time it said Deacon Red Berry.

I'll talk to him, but not now, Earl thought as he ignored this call.

Earl was happy, but he also knew he was in the middle of a shark tank and had no allies or supporters.

Earl leaned back in the big leather recliner that Pastor Harold always sat in. He listened to that little squeak that always happened right when he reached the 45 degree angle.

Earl sat up and wrote on a piece of paper, "Get somebody to fix this chair."

He could get a new chair, but there was something about sitting in Carter Luther Harold II's chair.

He then leaned back once more and the phone buzzed again.

The caller ID said Monique Pope.

Earl was intrigued. She probably wanted to keep her job as church secretary, but Earl thought she might be the perfect person to be his first ally.

He hit the button to accept the call.

"This is Minister, um, Pastor Ellington."

Earl smiled.

"Pastor Ellington. First, I wanted to congratulate you on your new position."

"Yes, thank you Sister Jones."

"And I wanted to let you know that if there is anything you need me to do for you, I would happily do it. I have been secretary at Arise for three years and Pastor Harold was never disappointed in any of my work. I am working on an associates in business at the—"

"Hold on, Sister Jones. I do not question your credentials."

"I just wanted to let you know that I am desirous of retaining my position as secretary. I assume there are a lot of people who want the job, but—"

"Sister Jones. Sister Jones, please calm down. I am not getting ready to make any changes at all. At least not right now."

Monique calmed down. She took a deep breath. She then said, "I'm happy to hear that. The real reason for my call, though, is that I had a pressing church matter that needs a signature from the pastor. Since you are now the pastor, I think we need to take care of this."

"Pressing church matter? It is 10:00 at night. Can this wait till tomorrow?"

"I am not sure if this can wait, Pastor."

Earl was overjoyed to hear someone call him Pastor. Not Minister. Not Reverend. Not Elder. But Pastor.

"Come by the office tomorrow. First thing. And we will take care of it," Earl said.

Earl wasn't sure what he could do about it anyway. He was desperately wanting some sleep and this was his first pastorate. He locked up at the church and left.

There were still a few stragglers around the church.

"Hey, Pastor."

"Good to see you, Pastor."

Earl still wasn't sure who was his real support and who wasn't, but he couldn't get past hearing people refer to him as Pastor.

The minutes to get home went by quickly, and soon he was in his apartment sitting at his kitchen table. Still with that stupid grin on his face.

A knock was at the door. He walked over and opened it. It was Carolyn Harold. She looked at him with a hurt and angry look.

"I didn't expect you," Earl said as Carolyn walked right in.

"What do you expect? You aren't answering your calls, and you said you want to marry me."

"Come on, girl, don't talk no stuff. You know this has been a busy day."

"Speaking of which, what was that all about?"

"What was what all about?" Earl answered.

"If you want someone who can preach, you vote for me and not Trey. I heard what you said."

Earl thought he had hidden his desire to step into the position.

"I don't know what you were listening to, but I didn't say that. Well, not exactly that."

"It's close enough. You stole my parents' church and my father's body ain't even cold."

"No, I'm the interim pastor."

"I said you were going to be all right, but you had to push it. Now you have started a war. A war you probably ain't ready to fight."

"What you talking 'bout now?"

"Red and Dex are gunning for you. The Harold family are gunning for you. Three-quarters of the church is gunning for you. You don't know what you are doing and now you have bogarted your way into a position you ain't fit for.

"The people want time to think while they decide on your brother or Dex."

"You stole my daddy's church. I don't know why my mother loved you so much."

"You loved me, too."

"Whatever."

There was another knock at the door and Earl opened it.

Monique walked in.

Carolyn uttered an expletive and said to Earl, "Oh no you ain't. So now you think you my daddy."

"Sister Jones here said there was some pressing matters to discuss, but I told her that she needs to wait till tomorrow," Earl said.

"Pressing matters to discuss? I suggest you get out of my face before I press my foot up your–" Carolyn said.

"Calm down, this is legitimate," Earl interrupted Carolyn.

He then turned to Monique and said, "What do you have to discuss?"

Monique stuttered.

"She ain't got nothing to discuss but how she was gonna do some things in here to you."

"Naw," Earl said.

"Let me tell you right now, I ain't my momma. I ain't sharing you with this trick or any other sista in that church."

"Trick? I'll show you trick." Monique approached Carolyn.

"You know what? If this is what you want. Go 'head. It's over, Earl." Carolyn said.

"What? No, baby. She has work. Ain't that right, Monique."

"Um," Monique said with a smile.

"I knew it. You want that then go the head on. Bye."

Monique said, "Bye."

"You better tell your girlfriend to act like she got some sense," Carolyn said as she walked out the door.

"So you ain't got no pressing business?"

"Come on, Earl, you know what this is about. It's approaching midnight and I called you wanting to meet. I just gave you an out, but you knew what this was about," Monique said as she eased in towards Earl.

Earl was torn. There was passion growing in him, but he also didn't want to start his pastorate off on such a raw note.

"So there is no pressing church business?"

"No, but—"

"OK, you have to go. And let me say this clearly: I will need your resignation in the morning. I will be looking for a new church secretary."

"But you said—"

"Bye, Monique."

Monique walked out the door.

Earl called Carolyn.

"So what do you want?" Carolyn answered.

"I want you to come over."

"Come over for what?"

"Come on, girl, stop playing. Anyway, you mind being an interim secretary for the interim pastor?"

Carolyn started laughing.

"'Cause Imma need some help with this thing," Earl said. "And in case you don't know, Monique is gone."

"Oh, I know."

"How do you know?"

"'Cause I'm sitting out here watching her drive off right now."

Then there was a knock at the door.

Earl opened it and Carolyn jumped in his arms. They kissed.

"I gotta go, but," she paused and looked him directly in the eyes, "I love you, Earl."

Earl smiled as she walked away.

"So you just stayed here to see what I was gonna do?"

"Naw, I knew what you was gonna do. I just wanted to be here to congratulate you for making the right choice."

Earl watched her get in her car and speed off.

CHAPTER 2

"If you throw your support behind me, I promise you an assistantship as well as preaching engagements throughout the country," Dex said to Earl as they sat in the pastor's office that Monday morning.

Earl leaned back in Pastor Harold's squeaky chair. He showed no response.

"Now come on, man. Trey can't promise you those speaking engagements. I make as much money on the road as I do in this church. Great preachers be makin' paper all over the country."

"Maybe that's why they didn't vote you in as pastor," Earl responded.

"How you figure?"

"Maybe they want a pastor who is in their church and not going somewhere else makin' paper," Earl said.

"Oh, so you feelin' yourself 'bout now, huh? You do know you ain't gonna be the permanent pastor?"

"From the look of the votes, neither will you."

Dex started to lose his patience.

"Now, Earl, you and I could turn this church around and start really making some noise in this city, but you in over your head. Come with me. Support me. And we will—"

"There ain't no way I'm supporting you. You want to know why?"

"'Cause you believe all the lies they say about me?"

Earl laughed. He said, "No. Because I know that the first day you get in office you will get rid of me."

"Come on, man, now that ain't true. You can trust—"

"I don't trust a word you saying and I think it is time we stopped pussyfooting 'round this. I don't trust you. I don't like you. I don't want you. So you are gone."

"What do you mean?"

"I mean you're gone."

"You can't do that."

"I'm the pastor."

"Interim pastor, and anyway, Red as the head of the trustees gotta OK that before it can go down."

"Well, I need to talk to Red then."

"You were right about one thing."

"Which is?" Dex asked.

"I need Red to do it. But Red and I are gonna fire you."

Dex walked out of the room.

Red walked by Dex and into the room.

"He says you are gonna fire me. Is that true?" Dex asked.

Red ignored him and said, "I have a meeting."

Dex stood there with his mouth open when Red closed the door in his face.

"You were right, that guy is a hot head," Earl said to Red.

Red laughed. "I told him if he didn't start treating me with respect I would get rid of him."

"Well, we got enough to get rid of him. He essentially attempted to bribe me. Did we get it all?"

"Oh yeah, this is the same mechanism we used to get rid of Carter. We even gave him a heart attack," Red said with a sinister laugh. He was referring to the death of the former pastor a few weeks before.

"Good." Earl responded.

"So this is point one in our four point plan to make you senior pastor."

"Get rid of Dex: check," Earl said.

"Now point two is to marry Carolyn Harold."

"That might be difficult. I have already tried, she says she ain't ready," Earl responded.

"You really gotta do this, Earl. It will drive a wedge. A lot of the Harolds' support will go to you, because you will be a Harold through marriage."

"But what can I do if she won't—"

"Ain't you been having relations with her? Just tell her you are gonna release the information if she doesn't come on and marry you. Church girls are scared of looking bad."

"Well not Carolyn."

"I don't care what you do. You just do it. Point three: 'Give Trey subordinate but important positions in the church.' We want to keep him busy in roles that are not primary."

"Any suggestions?"

"Are you the pastor or am I?"

"Um, how about director of youth operations this summer?"

"Naw, then the youth will love him. You know the youth are always the future," Red said.

"How 'bout over at the downtown mission?" Earl said.

"Now you're getting it. He will be out there barely scraping by while you will be strongly gaining support," Red said.

Earl nodded.

"Point 4, put off this vote for pastor until two or three years from now by running projects. We can't change pastors while we are in the middle of church projects, now can we?" Red laughed.

"You got it all figured out huh?" Earl said.

"Exactly. The one thing Dex said that is true is you are out of your league here. You need help. And I know you don't like her, but I think you should hire Monique back as secretary. Carolyn can't do the job."

"Didn't you just tell me to marry Carolyn and now you want me to hire back someone that will anger her?"

"The only way this is gonna work is if you have someone holding down the administrative angle of the church. Just tell Carolyn that you will never be alone with her."

Earl looked at Red.

Red continued, "You probably shouldn't be alone with her anyway, she is a bit enticing." Red laughed.

Red's phone rang.

He looked at it, laughed, and said, "It's the good Reverend Dwayne Dexter."

"Dex," Red said. The group looked on as he continued talking. "Calm down...Calm Down." Red continued. "Yeah, you know I'm talking to Earl...Well, I tend to agree with Earl. You may not be ready for..." Red then started yelling, "Man you ain't got the votes. The people don't want you. It is time to move on."

Earl could tell that there was some choice words being spewed by Dex.

"Just move on, it's time."

"That's it, I ain't gonna listen to this anymore."

The conversation continued.

"Oh you were gonna get rid of me? Well guess what, I got rid of you first."

Red hung up and said, "Old News."

"You think he is gonna hurt us?" Earl asked.

"How can he hurt us?" Red asked.

Earl shrugged.

"Well, Pastor Ellington, I have to do something now. Remember the four point plan and all of this will be permanently yours." Red reached his hands out.

Earl smiled.

"Even that squeaky chair that Carter would never get fixed."

Earl and Red laughed.

Red left.

Earl was happy things were coming together, but deep in his heart he knew that Red was not one who he could trust.

CHAPTER 3

"The phone has been ringing off the hook for the last day and you just now came to talk to me?" Lady Janet Harold said to her son as he stood in the doorway that Monday afternoon.

Lady Janet was cooking a double portion as she normally did to include her and her husband. She had yet to fully portion her meals correctly for one.

"I guess you found out that the church has made Earl Ellington the interim, giving the church time to discuss the matter," Trey responded.

"Have you talked to Earl?" Lady Janet asked.

"Not yet."

"Have you talked to Carolyn?"

"You know I don't like to talk to her to get to her boyfriend."

"Well, that trifling Monique has already been trying to move in on him," Lady Janet said.

"She has? How do you know?"

"Carolyn said it. I just want to know what's going on. Is Earl trying to pull one over on us?"

"What did Carolyn say?" Trey asked.

"She didn't know. Which is why I asked you what's going on."

"No, I, uh, I don't really know."

"You don't know," Lady Janet said in disgust.

"Carter's body ain't even cold yet and they gave the church to a child."

"Interim, not permanent."

"Are Dex and Red in on this? I bet you they had something to do with this. You need to do something to get control of this church," Lady Janet pressed.

"I ain't really into politics, Momma."

"That explains why you are sitting here with the most votes and somebody else is the pastor of your daddy's church," Lady Janet said.

Trey's mother was always the fire beneath the surface. She kind of stayed back, but Trey knew from experience that she was not one to roll over without a fight.

Trey said, "Let me go find out what's happening."

"And what are you going to do?"

"I'll, uh, go talk to a few—"

"You ain't got no idea, do you? I'm starting to wonder if Carter should have even made you pastor. You don't seem to have the stomach for it."

"Pops used to always say, 'Wait on the Lord. Let him decide.'"

Lady Janet sighed. She then put up her hand. "You can wait on the Lord by sitting down and doing nothing. Those people generally end up waiting forever and getting nothing."

"But Mom—"

"I ain't finished."

Trey threw his hands up in resignation.

Lady Janet continued, "And you can wait on the Lord by working hard and doing all that you can. These people generally end up in a better place whether they get what they desire or not."

Trey just continued looking at her.

"Which kind of waiting are you doing? I think you are lounging on the Lord, not waiting on the Lord. The devil is busy. Why ain't you?"

"It just happened yesterday. What do you want me to do?"

"Your daddy and I founded this church. This is our church. And you are just gonna watch Red and Dex take it away from you."

"This is God's church and I will wait on God to tell me what to do. God can take care of God's church," Trey said. He was not used to talking back to his mother, but he was more than a bit angry now.

Lady Janet looked angrily at Trey. She then stopped and smiled and laughed.

"Let me tell you what is gonna happen if you don't do something. Either Dex or Red have gotten to Earl and they will not allow the church to vote until Dex has all the votes. Or Earl has his own plans and will not allow the church to vote until he has the votes. You do realize that at least, don't you?" Lady Janet said.

"Let's let God be God and see what happens."

"Trey, do you even want to be pastor?"

"Huh? What kind of question is that?"

"I didn't stutter. Do you want to be pastor? 'Cause if you don't..."

"Of course I want the church, I have been called, and God placed me here. Daddy gave me a work to do. Yes, I want to be pastor."

"I'm not so sure."

"Mom, I gotta go. We need to talk about the funeral arrangements," Trey said.

"We will later. But I want you to really decide if you want it. 'Cause if you want it, you will have to fight for it," Lady Janet said.

Trey smiled and hugged his mother and said, "We don't need to talk about this now. Dad just died."

Lady Janet smiled and said, "Bye, baby."

"Bye, Mom."

Trey walked out of the house to the car. He knew his mother was on to something. There was a great struggle going on in that church.

Trey may have been in a verbal altercation with his mother, but he knew that he had not fully come to terms with accepting his father's charge to clean up that church. It wasn't in his nature to fight. He tried to, but he always wanted to take the less confrontational route in life.

He never asked himself fully, did he really even want the struggle to be pastor? He remembered his wife's question asking if ministry was even worth it. A question he had struggled with himself.

Trey asked himself if he was not fighting harder for the church because he was 'waiting on the Lord' or if it was because he really was hoping it would go to someone else.

These thoughts invaded his mind and struggled for supremacy. At the same time, he tried to think about what he was going to do. He formulated a plan to go straight to Earl and find out, if he could, whether Earl, Red, and Dex were up to something.

Trey picked up the phone and dialed Earl.

Earl answered, "Hello, Pastor Trey."

"We need to talk," Trey said.

"I've been waiting for your call."

They set up a time for their meeting.

CHAPTER 4

"Hello, Pastor Trey," Earl said.

Trey sensed a little bit of disrespect. He wasn't sure if it was because he was still trying to figure out Earl, or if Earl was disrespecting him.

It is quite common to use that kind of greeting in churches of other ethnicities. Even in multicultural settings they often call pastors things like Pastor Joe, or Pastor Mike. But in the black church, not so much.

"Minister Ellington," Trey said, specifically not identifying Earl as the pastor.

Trey knew that it was kind of hypocritical to be angered by Earl not referring to him as Pastor Harold, but then to not refer to Earl as Pastor Ellington. Trey rationalized in his mind that Ellington hadn't been ordained so he ain't got right to the title. Licensed, but not ordained.

"What can I do for you, Pastor?" Trey quickly answered.

"We need to talk about a few things. First, when do you plan on having the vote for pastor of the church? I have had a number of people telling me that we need to do this quickly so the church can move ahead."

"A lot of people who?"

"Well that isn't my point," Trey responded.

"I think we are going to disagree here."

"Disagree on what?" Trey asked.

"A few reasons. First of all the church is really at odds. There is no clear choice. Some in the church want Reverend Dexter to be pastor. Some of the church wants you to be pastor. And some of the church want me."

"Now come on, you had just a few more votes than TD Jakes got," Trey said while laughing. He immediately realized that he shouldn't have said that.

"You didn't get a majority," Earl said.

"Now hold on. I got the most votes of anyone. A clear plurality. A vote right now would show that I am the clear choice."

"Plurality ain't a majority. Besides, the church elected me interim. That means that I will do what's in the best interests of the church."

"The best interests of the church is to move forward and not hold this over their head," Trey interjected.

"Well that brings the next point. Why do you think the church will be doing nothing while we are deliberating?"

"What? What are you talking about?" Trey asked.

"At the next business meeting, I will introduce a couple of initiatives. The church has to be more active in the community and the church has to support and build good will."

"So you are going to move forward announcing initiatives?"

"Yep."

"Any of them major?" Trey asked.

"Everything that God does is major, Pastor."

"Will you stop speaking in riddles? Forget all of this. When are we going to have a vote on the next pastor?"

"When there is a clear majority of people requesting it. Until then, we will have regular discussions about the new pastor. In fact, I am about to create a pastoral search committee."

Trey felt like cursing but stifled the thought.

"So, Earl, do you want to be pastor?" Trey asked, completely throwing away any semblance of subtlety.

"If it is God's will."

"You ain't gonna get away with this, Earl," Trey said.

"I'm not gonna get away with what, helping the church navigate the waters until we get our next pastor?"

Trey immediately realized it would be a fight to get that vote to even happen.

"Minister Ellington, I just want you to do the right thing by the church and by the Harold family," Trey said.

"Pastor Trey, I just want to do the right thing by the church. And your family will always be taken care of. The first thing I want to do is offer my services to you as you plan your father's homegoing.

"And one of the first things I am going to do is create a 'founder's day' program to emphasize what your father has done for the church, community, and for many other ministers like you and myself," Earl said.

Trey was really starting to piece together who he thought Earl was.

"Pastor, I have a question for you," Earl said.

"What is it, Minister?"

"Who would you rather have as pastor of the church?" Earl began.

Trey sat quietly and with a bit of anxiety.

"Reverend Dexter or myself?"

Trey frowned up and said. "Why do you ask?"

"Because it may come down to that."

"What about me? I had the most votes by far," Trey said.

"You know, Pastor, I didn't have many votes, but no one knew I was in the running. I wonder how many votes I would get now."

"You would get what you got. This is my daddy's church and the people want a Harold."

Earl laughed. "So now it is you that will not answer clear questions."

"I will be the next pastor. You will not steal this. Not Dex, not you. I will be the next pastor. And the first thing I am gonna do when I clean this up is get rid of you for trying to play games with God's church," Trey said confidently.

"I'm confused. You said it is your daddy's church. You said it is your church. Now you saying it is God's church. Which is it, Trey?"

"God is the shepherd and the Harold family are the under-shepherds."

"If that is the case, then why am I pastor right now and you are begging me for a vote?"

Trey lost it and began yelling. "You are gone. You're gone, man. What's the matter with you?"

"Nothing is wrong with me. You are the one yelling."

Trey then fought back the urge to continue yelling. He calmed down and said, "We will vote you out. We will vote me in. And then the church will move forward."

There was a brief silence and then Earl said, "If that is God's will, then it will be done."

Trey was about to say something else, but he simply responded, "Bye, Minister."

"Bye, Pastor Trey," Earl said.

Trey hung up.

CHAPTER 5

Earl and Deacon Red Berry were sitting in the Pastor's Office waiting for the first staff meeting since Earl had taken over to begin.

Red was standing while Earl was seated, leaning back and looking up as Carter Harold II used to do when he was pastor.

Red said, "Hey, I got a new major initiative that is gonna solidify you in as pastor."

Earl leaned further back in the big leather chair and asked, "What is it?"

Red smiled and said, "With all the turmoil going on in this church, I called up a few of my friends to sell them on a reality TV show."

"Huh?" Earl asked.

"Yeah, think about it. A church brought through the mud by its former pastor's indiscretions, but now the church is put on the right footing. A former rival attempts to derail his attempts to do God's will, and the child of the pastor stands in your way."

"So you think Dex and Trey will go along with it?" Earl asked.

"Who cares? If Dex don't go along with it, we will simply replace him with some other guy."

"Replace him? You mean get somebody else to fight me for leadership?"

"It's TV, man. We'll just hire an actor. I got my eye on a preacher across town who I bet would love to come in and play the part," Red responded.

"So you have thought about this."

"Listen here, young-blood, I have thought through everything."

"OK, so what about Trey? You can't just replace him."

"Leave it to me. I will sell it to the Harold family. Now stop interrupting the story." Red laughed.

"This is the chronicle of how a new, young, outsider took this church to the next level by following God's will."

Earl started smiling at this point. "So you already have some network executives?"

"Yeah, but we need to record a pilot. And they want to start soon."

"How soon?"

"Now soon."

"What are you talking about, Deacon?"

"I am saying that I have a couple cameramen ready to record this minister's meeting in a few minutes."

"What? I don't know—"

"Before you say no, think about it. Nobody has done this. You will be the first. Think about the exposure for you and for the church."

"What are you gonna get out of this?"

Red took a step back and said, "I'm gonna get a pastor who I can work with."

"OK," Earl said in resignation.

In his heart he was already thinking about how he would look on TV and how this could push him into the revival circuit in a way like he never imagined.

Earl smiled as Red continued talking.

"I wanted to call it 'Rising from the Ashes.' However, somebody wanted to call it 'Broken Saints.'"

"Broken Saints? What are they trying to say? What's so broken about this church?" Earl interrupted.

Red laughed. "I can see you having a problem with calling it Saints, but you gotta admit, there is a whole lot of dysfunction up in here."

"Ain't nobody tried to shoot nobody up in here like I heard happened somewhere else. Ain't nobody interrupted church with some foolishness up in here."

Red continued laughing. "I interrupted church myself. But who cares what they call it. This is going to solidify you as pastor as well as get us some big time TV exposure. You betta get your sermons together, Earl, 'cause you are gonna be huge."

Earl calmed down and a smile emerged on his face. "You right, Deacon. Good idea."

At that point Dex walked in. A minute later, Trey walked in.

Then a couple cameramen walked into the room taking footage.

"What's this?" Dex asked.

"We are recording a reality show," Red said.

Dex smiled and turned to one of the cameras to talk.

Trey said, "What, we didn't vote for this."

"I, as the pastor, authorized this," Earl said.

"You are not the pastor. You are the interim pastor," Trey said.

Red had a look of concern on his face and turned to one of the cameras and said, "Are you questioning the wisdom of the church that elected Minister Ellington here as pastor?"

Trey's nose flared and he said, "No one elected Earl as pastor–"

"Reverend Harold, I think you should show more respect to the pastor of the church while he is in an official capacity running this meeting," Red said.

"Why are you talking like that, Red? You playing to the cameras?" Trey asked.

"I think it is a good idea. We have the cameras rolling to show the transfer of power in a church. When are we going to have this election?" Dex asked.

"We have not set a date for that. I don't think we need to rush this," Earl said.

"We must be careful not to run ahead of the Lord. It will happen when it needs to happen, but while we are waiting, we will continue moving forward. Ain't that right, pastor?" Red said to Earl.

"Exactly. Plus we have a lot of things to do as we take our church to the next level," Earl continued.

Trey turned and looked at the camera and said, "How long do you plan on these cameras being here?"

"Ahh, don't worry about them, Reverend, just be yourself," Red said.

"So you saying you ain't gonna have a vote any time now? I ain't feelin' this," Dex said.

"The people voted a pastor until they vote a new pastor," Red said.

"I don't think the people are going to be happy with what you are trying to do here," Trey said.

"What? The people aren't gonna be happy that the person they elected as pastor exercising the rights of being pastor?" Red said.

"OK, what are we here for, Earl?" Trey asked.

"Reverend, the first thing I want to do is create a pastoral search committee."

"That's what I'm talking 'bout," Dex said.

"On the committee is Deacon Red Berry, myself, and mother Earlene Williams."

"And how did you come up with this group?" Trey asked.

"God told me to do it, Reverend."

"The next order of business, I wanted to give you two your assignments," Earl said.

"Assignments? I have a lot of speaking engagements that I need to complete over the next few months," Dex said.

"Well, the church needs you here. I am assigning you to work with the children's Sunday School."

Red stifled a laugh.

"I can't do it."

"You can do it or I will accept your resignation from church employ."

"What are you talking about? I have a lot of responsibilities." Dex said.

"You are gone every week. The only time we see you is when we want to elect officers. We ain't got no time any longer for this," Earl said.

Dex looked at Trey and asked, "Are you cool with this?"

"Well, you are always gone."

Dex cursed and knocked some materials off the table and left.

Red turned his head to be in line with a camera and said, "Wow, we sure dodged a bullet when we didn't elect him as pastor."

"You weren't saying that when you were trying to force him down our throat as pastor," Trey said.

"And Reverend Harold, our downtown mission needs help. I think you ought to go work there full time for the time being."

Trey laughed. "So I see the game. You are trying to get rid of Dex by forcing him to stay in the church and you are trying to get rid of me by forcing me to stay out of the church."

"No, Reverend, I think these moves are the best for the ongoing work of God."

"OK, I'll do it, but you need to set a date for the next election," Trey said.

"That will be the first thing on the agenda when the pastoral search committee meets," Earl responded.

Trey got up and left.

Earl looked over at Red and said, "That went very well."

Red looked at a camera and said, "Let us pray for a great move of God in this church." He bowed his head and began to pray.

CHAPTER 6

Sunday morning came quickly, more quickly than usual as the anticipation of a new regime took hold of the church.

Earl powerfully closed his sermon that Sunday morning.

Dex's face demonstrated that he wasn't really into the sermon. He reluctantly stood in support of the final point.

Trey's countenance was not much better.

Both were waiting for the time that Earl would address all the cameras all over the church as well as when the church would have the election.

Earl then gave the benediction and walked up to Trey and said, "Why don't you and Reverend Dexter greet the members. I am feeling a little under the weather."

"Are you gonna make any announcements? What are you doing?" Dex said.

"I have to go. We will announce what we need to announce at Wednesday Bible study."

"You mean when nobody is here?" Dex said.

"Instead of talking about why ain't nobody here, why ain't you brought nobody?" Earl answered.

Dex snickered, "We gonna get rid of your smug behind."

"Whose we?" Earl asked while looking at Trey.

"I ain't with him, but I ain't with you either," Trey said.

"Just stop making the members wait. I gotta go," Earl said as he rushed off the podium toward the back of the church.

Trey saw his sister Carolyn rush into the back following Earl.

Trey and Dex walked to the back of the church.

Dex laughed. "I think you and I need to stop fighting and start recognizing who our real enemy is."

"And who might that be?" Trey said as they both continued walking down the aisle to the back of the church.

The two didn't look at each other but continued speaking as they walked.

The two were then at the door shaking hands with parishioners. They continued speaking to one another between greetings with members.

"When are we gonna vote?" One of the mothers of the church asked Trey.

"I hope it will be soon," Trey said.

"Sister, pray that God will make it happen," Dex said to her.

A few others asked as well, but Trey noted that there was not a lot of people expressing a desire for this vote to happen soon.

More people were interested in the cameras.

One brother asked, "What are all of these cameras for?"

Trey answered, "The interim pastor will tell us on Wednesday."

Dex answered, "The interim pastor is trying to turn this church into the Real Housewives of Atlanta."

The brother looked at him funny and then left.

"I should have known you couldn't keep your mouth closed," Trey said to Dex under his breath.

"I can't believe you're listening to that guy. Come on, man, you ain't dumb, you know that guy is scheming to keep your daddy's church."

"Yeah, and you know good and well you don't care about me having my daddy's church," Trey answered.

They stopped bickering long enough to shake a few more hands.

Dex then said with a snicker, "You right. I don't want you to have your daddy's church. But you and I both have an interest in forcing a church vote. Now I want them to vote for me. You want them to vote for you. But we both want a vote."

"And how are you gonna force a vote?"

"Now we getting somewhere. Let's talk."

Trey looked Dex in his eyes and said, "You know what? I don't want the church if it means I have to scheme with the likes of you."

Trey shook a few more hands and then said, "I think we are through. Bye, Reverend, and God bless."

Dex mocked Trey, "God bless." Dex then said, "See, I was gonna give you a good place in my administration, but now you blew it."

Trey laughed. He walked back into the sanctuary and searched for his wife before he left the church.

Carolyn got to the back room where she saw Red and Earl talking to a black woman in a suit that she didn't know.

"Oh, this is gonna be gold. You, sir, are a great preacher. You are ready for TV," the woman said to Earl, who was beaming.

"I told ya. I told ya. This is gonna be great," Red said.

"Oh, and this here is the next first lady of the church," Red continued, while motioning over to Carolyn.

The attractive black woman looked at Carolyn and said, "Oh yes, this is gonna work. She is beautiful. What did you say Red, middle of next season we will have a wedding?"

"Wedding, who said anything 'bout a wedding?" Carolyn said.

"Yes, I, uh, only if you are ready," Earl said.

"What are you talking about?"

Red looked over at Earl and asked, "I thought you said she was on board."

"On board for what?" Carolyn said now as her voice was getting louder.

"Hello, Lady Carolyn Harold, my name is Shanice Jackson. The Deacon here invited me in to help the church get the TV show off the ground."

"TV Show? You mean you are going to put our church service on television?" Carolyn asked.

Red gave Earl an angry look and then turned to Carolyn and said, "No, we are going to have a reality show."

"Reality show?"

"Yes, a reality show chronicling this church's rise from the ashes."

"So in this reality show we have Earl as pastor, and you said I'm getting married," Carolyn said.

Red looked back at Earl, who turned away with a sheepish look.

"And when were you gonna tell me I was gonna get married?" Carolyn asked Earl. "I'm sorry, Ms. Jackson, I am not engaged to Earl and he is not the pastor of the church. He is not even the top candidate to become pastor. He is the interim."

"I have a contract signed by the head of your Trustees and your interim pastor that tells me he is your pastor," Shanese said.

"Well, I am not engaged to him, so I don't know how you gonna have a wedding," Carolyn continued.

"Even better, we can have some sub plots of the pastor finding a wife," Shanese said.

"Or maybe we can bring Monique in here," Red said.

"Monique? I ain't trying to hear nothing 'bout no Monique," Carolyn said.

"No, we are dating, we aren't engaged, but we are serious," Earl said to both Carolyn and Shanese.

"Well, it doesn't really matter."

"What do you mean it doesn't matter? You said it is a reality show," Carolyn asked.

"We make the reality. We may not even need the engagement," Shanese said.

"So, Earl, when are you going to allow the church to vote on the next pastor?" Carolyn asked.

"No, stop, this needs to be on camera. Where is a cameraman?" Shanese said.

"I ain't saying nothing on camera," Carolyn said angrily as she left.

Her mind was swirling with the thoughts of her boyfriend scheming to force her to marry him as well as scheming to take the church.

She wasn't sure what to believe or what to do, but she at least knew that she didn't want to marry him now.

CHAPTER 7

"What mess have you gotten me into, Red?" Shanese asked Red before the Wednesday night Bible study.

Red smiled and said, "I don't know what you're talking about."

"The network thinks they are getting a show that hardly looks like what is happening here. The pastor is not the pastor."

"Interim pastor is still pastor," Red interrupted.

"The pastor ain't getting married, so we don't have a wedding episode."

"We can work around that. By the way, we have a funeral."

"Funeral?" Shanese said while her face frowned up. She continued, "You lied to me, and I sold the network on your lie."

Red smiled. "We are gonna give them something better than they thought they were getting."

Shanese rolled her eyes and said, "And what is that?"

"In due time," Red said as he and Shanese watched Terry Smith direct the choir.

"He might be a star," Shanese said as she pointed to Terry.

Dex walked up to the two as they stood watching the choir practice.

"Ms. Jackson," Dex said as Red ignored him.

"Yes?" Shanese said.

"I am the assistant pastor and the next pastor of–" Dex continued.

Red laughed. "This right here is old news."

"I don't know about that," she said to Red as she began to look at Dex. "He looks like he could be helpful to us."

"We already have the battle for pastor between Trey and Earl. We already have the relationship angle as Earl and Carolyn attempt to become a couple. We already have—"

"You don't have a wedding, you don't have a pastor," Shanese said.

"Not to mention neither of them two guys can preach," Dex said.

"So what are you doing? Pitching me on getting on my show?" Shanese asked Dex.

"You need me on your show. I don't know if Red has told you anything about—"

"I ain't told her a thing about you because you are old news. You ain't gonna be long on the pastoral staff. Why don't you go find somewhere else to—"

"Hold on, it's coming to me," Shanese said as she looked up.

Shanese looked at Dex closely.

"Yeah, you are good with the ladies, ain't ya?" she asked.

Before Dex could answer, she responded.

"Yeah, how about we take this guy—"

"Dwayne Dexter," Dex interrupted.

Shanese shot Dex a look that told him never to interrupt her again.

She then continued, "Reverend Dexter here can be the proverbial Ministerial ladies man."

"We don't need a ladies man, we got—"

"Earl is a college boy and Trey is a choir boy. No we gonna need someone like Mr. Dexter here."

Dex smiled slyly, as if trying to figure out where this conversation was going.

Shanese continued, "Let him chase the women while Trey and Earl fight over the pastorate."

"No, but I am going to be the next pastor," Dex said.

Shanese looked at him and said, "You want to know what part you are gonna play in my show? You are the ladies' man. Now go find some ladies and get out of my face."

"I thought you said this was a reality show," Dex said.

"I make reality," Shanese said.

Red snickered. "You got a part now. So move on."

Dex stood there as if he had been hit in the stomach.

Shanese turned to Red and started talking about Terry.

"Now this guy, we have to really think about how we are going to fit him in. Can't have a show about the Black church without a homosexual choir director," Shanese said.

Dex was still standing there and Shanese said, "Will you get out of my face, man?"

Dex dropped his head and slowly walked away.

"You were saying," Red said after Dex left.

"I want to talk to him. Terry. Let's get him on board."

Red walked over to the Terry and whispered in his ear.

Terry yelled to the choir, "Lois, come take over for a few."

Lois walked up to direct as Terry and Red walked back to Shanese.

"Minister Terry Smith is our minister of music," Red said to Shanese.

"This is sister Shanese Jackson. She is going to–"

"Shanese Jackson, producer of the Genuine Wives of Atlanta. It is great to meet you," Terry said while shaking her hand.

"Ahh, so you watch my shows?" Shanese asked.

"Atlanta, Thugs of Detroit, and the Brothers of Compton. I have seen them all. And now you are going to turn our church into a hit show?" Terry smiled.

Shanese smiled and turned to Red. "Yes, I think we have found the next star."

She then said to Terry, "We need to set up an appointment to talk to you and your choir."

"You got a boyfriend?" Shanese asked.

Terry looked around and said, "I, uh, that would be wrong..." He then looked at Red and said, "Wouldn't it?"

"I'll close my ears," Red said.

Terry stood there for a couple seconds.

"Oh yeah, I forgot, church folks can clap at your music, but they send you to hell after the song is over."

Terry continued looking confused.

Shanese continued. "Don't worry, we will find out all we need to find out. Welcome aboard." Shanese shook Terry's hand.

Terry walked back to the choir.

"So we got our ladies' man. We got our gay sidekick. Now you are gonna have to get me in good with either Trey or Earl. Preferably both," Shanese said to Red.

"Before we get to that, I think you need to talk to the first lady. Lady Janet."

CHAPTER 8

"What are you doing?" an exasperated Lady Janet said.

Trey continued eating his meal calmly.

Beverly, Trey's wife, looked at Janet and said, "He is always so calm."

"Just like his father," Janet said while jabbing at some pasta and putting it in her mouth.

"What do you want me to do?" Trey asked.

"I want you to fight for it. Your father didn't start this church for Red to take it," Janet continued.

"There is nothing I can do. I will just go work with the children and—"

"Don't tell me you are gonna let that snotty nosed kid assign you to the bottom of the barrel."

"My pastor gave me the assignment, and I will do it."

Janet took another bite and then after composing herself said, "They are turning the church into a joke. Some woman named Shanese Jackson called and wants a meeting."

"What did she want?" Trey asked.

"She wants to talk about the TV show they are turning the church into."

"She called me too," Beverly said.

"What?" Janet asked.

"Yes, they called me and I have a meeting later this week."

"OK, we need to discuss how we are going to handle this," Janet said.

"I told them I ain't meeting with them. I am going to leave it in the hands of God." Trey said.

Janet threw up her hands and Beverly rolled her eyes.

"God don't expect you to do nothing. You can't expect God to do anything for you when you ain't doing nothing for yourself," Janet said.

"Dad said—"

"Your father said to take care of the church and the church is going to hell," Janet said.

"Dad said to do it the right way. I want to do it the right way."

Janet looked at Beverly and said, "Will you talk some sense into your husband?"

Beverly snickered and said, "I can't talk any sense into your son."

Trey continued eating.

"Well, how about you and I talk about how we are going to handle Ms. Shanese Jackson?" Janet said to Beverly.

"That sounds good. What do you have in mind?" Beverly asked.

"For one thing, I will show up at your meeting. And let's go in there with our ideas on how this show should go."

"I don't think we need to get into this," Trey said.

"You can do what you're gonna do," Beverly said.

"Which is nothing," Lady Janet interjected.

"But we are going to plan how this will work." Beverly said.

"Weren't you the one who wondered if we should even do ministry?" Trey asked.

"Yes, but if we are gonna do it, we are gonna do it right."

"I'm glad you married a smart woman," Lady Janet said.

Trey went back to eating.

"I appeared on the Wives of Atlanta show once. My friend Ebony Lewis invited me to a party once," Janet said.

"You are friends with Ebony?" Beverly said.

"You know Ebony?"

"Well, from the show. She is the star. Took it over ever since she joined in the fourth season."

"So you watch it?"

"I watch every episode. I'm surprised you didn't see it."

"Well they said my scene ended up on the cutting room floor, but I still made a nice chunk of change just for being on the show."

"I told Beverly to turn that mess off, but she is hooked on that madness," Trey interjected.

"Well, I don't want to be on the show," Janet said, picking up her phone and dialing, "but if we are gonna be on the show..."

She finished dialing and put the phone on the table next to her plate as all three heard the phone ring.

Janet then said, "...we need to be READY to be on the show."

"Janet, girl, why it took you so long to call me?" Ebony Lewis said through the phone. Her voice was immediately recognizable to everyone.

"Well hello to you too, Ebony," Janet said.

Ebony laughed. "I know this is serious for the first lady to call me."

"I have my son and his wife Beverly here."

"Little Trey over there? Hey, Trey," Ebony said.

"Good to hear you, Ms. Ebony," Trey said before going back to eating.

Lady Janet continued, "Shanese Jackson is about to turn our church into a reality show and I know you know how to handle this."

"Bye, Ms. Ebony. I don't want to be involved in any of this scheming," Trey said as he stood up.

"Mom, I'm going to the church to begin the work the pastor assigned to me," he said as he left.

"Bye, Trey," Ebony said through the phone.

"Don't mind him. He is as hardheaded as his daddy," Janet said.

"So have you met with Shanese yet?"

"No," Beverly said.

"Good, when you meet with her, she is gonna try to pigeonhole you into a character. See, when I started on Genuine Wives of Atlanta, she wanted me to be the 'homely, everything is great, love your husband' woman. I did it for a little while, but then he cheated on me."

"I remember that. You were having dinner parties," Beverly said.

"Well, they still used old videos to keep it looking like I was still that girl. I had to threaten to leave before they would give me a part to play that was more in line with my real self."

"Part to play?" Janet asked. "I thought this was reality TV."

"One thing you will learn soon is that the only thing real about reality TV is your name."

"So what do you suggest we do?" Beverly asked.

"I suggest you and Janet get a role you want to play that you will pitch to her. Otherwise, she will put you in a role, and I doubt you will like what she gives you. Nobody does," Ebony said.

"What do you mean by role?"

"Look at her shows. She always has a fool. She always has a ladies man. She always has the fat friend. Find a role you can play and tell her you will play it," Ebony said.

"And what about Trey?"

"You better get him on board, otherwise he ain't gonna like what this show makes him look like. Remember Ken from season 3?"

"Yeah, the juvenile delinquent."

"Well in real life he was a star student. Right now he is trying to live down the damage to his life that happened on the show."

"I thought he had a few DUIs and some drug charges?"

"Look it up. They all came to nothing. I told you, reality TV ain't reality. At least Shanese Jackson's version of reality TV isn't," Ebony said.

"OK, so Beverly and I will start thinking about our personas."

"What about Carolyn? She really needs to be here as well," Ebony said.

"Well, I'm not sure about Carolyn. Her boyfriend is trying to steal the church from our family," Janet said.

"Wow, your church really is a reality show." Ebony laughed.

"Shut up, girl," Lady Janet said.

"We are trying to get the church to Trey where it belongs," Beverly said.

"Well, I gotta go, but you two really need to have your ducks in a row before you talk to Shanese."

"Will do," Janet said.

"Call me next week. Since you're now in a reality show, I need to talk to you about getting on the Genuine Wives. Let me know when that funeral is so I can get there."

"Bye, girl," Janet said. She hung up the phone.

"OK, it's time to get serious," Janet said to Beverly.

CHAPTER 9

"I am sick and tired of this no count Negro," Carolyn Harold said to Shanese.

They sat in Shanese Jackson's office. Red had turned Dex's office into a temporary one for Shanese.

"This right here, you are gonna have to articulate on camera," Shanese answered.

"What are you talking about?"

"Your man—"

"He ain't my man no mo'," Carolyn said.

Shanese stopped and then said carefully, "Pastor Ellington—"

"He ain't the pastor," Carolyn interrupted again.

"Come on, girl, you and I both know who I'm talking about."

"Yeah, I know who you talking bout. And he ain't the pastor."

"Earl," Shanese said and then smiled.

Carolyn looked at her angrily.

"This church has a lot of decisions to make. We are in the middle of the old and the new. And you are a part of both," Shanese said.

"How so?"

"Your boyfriend–" Shanese began to say.

"Ex," She said quickly before Carolyn could interrupt.

"Is the new pasto..."

"Interim pastor." Shanese said.

"Uh huh," Carolyn said.

"So you are a part of the new, but you and your family are the founders and a strong part of the old," Shanese continued.

"Ms. Jackson, why do you want to talk to me?"

"You are the key. I think your relationship with Earl could be a strong part of this show."

Carolyn looked at Shanese and then her hardened look slowly brightened.

"I don't see how. We aren't dating anymore. He lied to me. He tried to force me into some kind of marriage that I didn't want. And anyway, I'm supporting my brother to be the next pastor, so I'm part of the old."

"Even if that is true, I know you still have feelings for Earl."

"And how do you know that? I don't even know you, so how do you know me?"

"Let me rephrase that. You probably have some feelings. You dated for over a year."

"And how do you know that?"

"I do my research. I even know that you are the holdup and he wanted to marry you."

Carolyn looked shocked. "Who told you that?"

"Research. Now, I think this season has a number of strong story lines in it. From your flamboyant choir director and his attempts to hide his sexuality by dating women—"

"Terry has been delivered from that."

Shanese looked at Carolyn with a knowing grin and said, "Everybody's been delivered."

"God can do it."

Shanese ignored her and continued.

"Next the assistant pastor who is always chasing women."

Carolyn looked mad.

"Don't worry, I'm talking bout Dwayne Dexter. Your man only has eyes for you."

"He is not my man," Carolyn said.

Shanese continued.

"To the old guard attempting to take back the church. Your sister-in-law, brother, and your mother."

"And me," Carolyn interrupted.

"Maybe, but the real story is how you and Earl navigate your relationship while in the middle of all this church drama. That is the show Broken Saints, and I think I can sell it."

Carolyn thought for a moment about it and said, "Mom and Trey ain't gonna go for turning this into no mess."

"The pastor and the head of the Trustees are good with it, so your mom needs to get with the program."

"So you got it all figured out?"

"You don't get the number one reality show in the country without figuring it all out," Shanese said and then laughed.

"So I ask again, what you want with me?"

"I need your relationship with Earl to at least last through the end of the year."

"I told you it's over."

"If your relationship lasts until the end of the year, I guarantee that you will be a star. Hell, I might even get you a spin-off. Now, Red promised me a wedding show—"

"I ain't marrying that fool. I told you—"

Shanese interrupted her. "Since that ain't happening, maybe we can get you a show about the real church girls. 'Cause I know for a fact yall ain't as pure and holy as you trying to make me think. How about four or five of your friends on a show?"

Carolyn smiled. She then said, "So you are telling me that all I have to do is play along and you will get me my own show?"

Shanese looked at her and said, "I think I can swing that."

Carolyn reached out her hand and shook Shanese's hand then said, "You have a deal."

Shanese smiled and said, "Now I have a meeting with your mother and your sister-in-law. I got just the parts for them to play."

"What about Trey?"

"Trey is gonna make it hard, but everybody has a price," Shanese answered.Is there anything you think I should know before talking to them?" Shanese continued.

"Why do I get the idea that you are trying to pump me for information to use against my family?" Carolyn said.

"Probably because I am trying to pump you for information that I can use against your family," Shanese said.

"I'm gonna work with you, but there is nothing I will do that will jeopardize my family or my family's church. That is the most important thing to us."

"Thank you."

"Thank you for what?"

"For telling me the most important thing to them. It is going to make this discussion easier."

Carolyn looked at Shanese and then said, "Girl, bye."

Shanese smiled.

CHAPTER 10

"I think we have enough for the show." Shanese said to Red as they both sat in Shanese's temporary office at the church.

"I still need to talk to Lady Janet, but we have a show."

"So what do we have to do now?" Red said as he showed a big toothy grin.

"Nothing. My people are already recording everything. We have a couple worship services and just about every meeting of the church recorded. We even recorded a bake sale and bingo night," Shanese said while laughing.

Monique Jones came to the door and walked in. She looked at Red with a bit of disdain and then turned to Shanese and said, "Lady Janet is here to meet with you."

"What is Monique doing here? Earl fired her," Red asked.

"I hired her as my secretary. We need as much information as we can get."

"But I gave you as much information as you need," Red said as he frowned.

"You know what? I have a meeting and I don't really need to run my personnel decisions by you," Shanese said to Red.

Red looked like he had been hit in the gut.

"Monique, please show Mr. Berry the door."

"I know the way out of here," Red said as he stood up.

Monique snickered.

Red walked out.

Lady Janet and Beverly Harold walked into the room.

"Lady Janet, thank you for coming," Shanese said as she reached to shake Lady Janet's hand.

Lady Janet shook it and looked around. "You have done a lot to this choir room."

Shanese smiled and said, "The reason why I wanted to talk to you is—"

"We know why you want to talk to us. You want to tell us what parts to play in your TV show, but we only play the parts that we should play," Lady Janet said.

"You misunderstand. This is a reality show. We do not want you to play any parts," Shanese said.

"It appears that you tell different people different things, Ms. Jackson. Everyone is saying that reality TV ain't reality," Beverly said.

"And what is that supposed to mean?"

"Here is what is gonna happen. You are going to help us make Trey pastor of this church and we will help you make a great television show," Lady Janet said.

Shanese smiled and said, "I already have a great television show."

"Red, Dex, and Earl are not the stuff of great TV," Beverly said.

"Well, since we're being honest, neither is your snoozer of a husband Trey. Out of all of the assistants, he is probably the last one I would make a show out of," Shanese said.

Lady Janet and Beverly both looked shocked.

"OK, now that we are through playing, Lady Janet, you are the matriarch struggling with the reality that your church needs to move away from your family to your son-in-law." Shanese said.

"Son-in-law? Earl ain't marrying Carolyn."

"Maybe, or maybe not."

"What's that supposed to mean?" Beverly said.

Shanese continued, "And you are the jilted first lady who always wanted to be a first lady and will now have to come to the realization that her sister-in-law is now going to take the crown."

"That doesn't even remotely resemble reality," Beverly said.

"Weren't you the one who just told me that reality TV ain't got nothing to do with reality?" "Ebony told me she talked to you."

"What?" Lady Janet said.

"Don't be mad at her. Pretty soon you and I are gonna be tight like that. You are gonna tell me when somebody is trying to pull something over my eyes."

"I doubt that," Lady Janet replied.

"Anyway, I just care about the bottom line. I care about a better TV show. That's all. I don't care about Red, Dex, or anybody else. I just want what makes a good TV show. Everybody else in this church wants something from you. Even your daughter-in-law sitting there."

Beverly looked at Shanese angrily.

"But I like you, Lady Janet. You are like me."

"How am I like you?" Lady Janet said.

"We both rose up with or without traditional power. You are a leader in this church and you haven't been elected to anything. In a different world at a different time, you would probably be the senior pastor of this church."

Lady Janet fought back a smile. She said, "Now wouldn't that be something?"

"I'm gonna be frank. I need you. I need Trey. I don't need Beverly," Shanese continued.

"Why are you attacking me?"

"I'm not attacking you. I have looked around this church. I see you have no power in this church."

"And who, according to you, has power in this church?"

"Trey. He has some kind of intangible power that some church folks might call the Holy Ghost. I would just say he has some kind of non-traditional charisma that I can't put my finger on. 'Cause he is a boring guy. I don't know how you put up with being with somebody who ain't got no swag at all," Shanese said.

"Lady Janet, you have a hold on the church. Some of it is your grace, and some of it is just time spent in the church."

"Red has a tenuous hold on the church," Shanese continued. "I don't trust him, I don't know if anybody does, but he has some support in the church.

"Dex is a joke. No one takes him seriously. That was Red's big mistake when he allied himself with that fool." Shanese continued. "Earl is the Johnny-come-lately that nobody knows but everybody thinks is better than Dex." "And Terry. Everybody on all sides love the guy, even though they paradoxically hate his homosexuality." Shanese said.

Shanese stopped talking.

"So you got it all figured out," Lady Janet said.

"Not yet, but I soon will. Your son may be the right person to pastor this church, I don't know, and frankly, I don't care. All I care about is that he is the wrong person to build a show on."

"Why are you acting like we all want to be on your television show?" Beverly asked.

"Didn't you come in here wanting to tell me which parts you were going to play on my show?" Shanese asked.

Lady Janet stood up and reached out to shake Shanese's hand and said, "Ms. Jackson, my son will be pastor of this church or we don't have anything to talk about."

Shanese shook Lady Janet's hand again and said, "Then it appears we have nothing to talk about."

Lady Janet and Beverly walked out the door.

Shanese picked up her phone and called the network.

She said, "Full speed ahead."

She sat in her chair and smiled.

CHAPTER 11

After Wednesday night Bible study, Shanese walked up to Trey.

"Why are you ignoring me?" Shanese asked.

"'Cause I got nothing to talk to you about," Trey responded.

"We need to talk about access to your ministry if this show is gonna work," Shanese said.

"I ain't gonna play games with the Lord's church, Ms. Jackson," Trey said to Shanese.

Shanese looked at Trey up and down. She could quickly and easily figure out what folks wanted that she could use.

But Trey appeared to have no weaknesses.

On the other hand, Shanese had been around long enough to know that everybody had a weakness.

"I ain't asking you to 'play games.' I'm asking you to—"

"Please, I talked to my mother and wife. I talked to Terry and Lois. Dex and Red been sending me text messages. Yeah, I know you playing games," Trey said calmly.

Shanese smiled.

Shanese realized that she wasn't gonna be able to snow Trey.

"You know what, I'm gonna be honest with you."

"OK, now we are getting somewhere."

"I am creating a TV show. And I want the best show. That is what I want," she said.

Trey crossed his arms in front of him.

"And because I want a good show. I want you in it."

"So you want a boring preacher who can't preach in your show?" Trey said.

"I didn't say you can't preach—"

"But you said I was boring."

"Does that anger you?" Shanese asked.

Trey laughed. He then said, "You can get out of here with those mind games."

Shanese began to lose her temper and asked angrily, "What do you want?"

"I want God's will for this church."

"How do you know this show ain't God's will?"

"I don't know, but, um, er..."

"Ah, there it is, Pastor. How do you know that God ain't using this to get your next pastor?" Shanese drove the point further home.

Trey looked at her. She could tell he was trying to figure out a good answer to the question, but he couldn't.

Shanese laughed. She thought, *Check mate.*

"God used a donkey in the Bible, so if God spoke through a donkey, I suppose God could use your television show," Trey said.

That comment erased Shanese's smile.

"The interim pastor gave his ok to the show, so I will not disrupt it," Trey said. "But I ain't gonna help you make a mockery of this situation," Trey continued.

"And if there is nothing else, we have a minister's meeting soon," he said.

Shanese smiled and said, "Yes, I am also invited to this meeting."

"You are invited to the meeting? Well then, I will see you there."

Trey stood up and walked out of her office. He immediately saw Dex standing out in the lobby.

"Reverend Harold, I have been wanting to talk to you, man. Where you been?"

Trey said, "What do you want?"

"I need to talk to you about this television show. I don't know for sure if this is the best thing for our church and–"

Trey laughed. "So things ain't going the way you think they should and now you asking me to drop you a lifeline?"

Dex leaned in to Trey and whispered, "They are gonna force Earl down our throat as pastor. I think you and I have something to work together on."

"Work together? I already told you I ain't working with you. You don't work with anyone else. You ain't worked with anyone when you tried to steal the church, did you? We ain't got nothing to work together about."

"That's all water under the bridge."

Trey stopped walking, turned to Dex, and said, "I want to be pastor. I really do. But if it ain't me, I would vote for Earl long before I would vote for you."

Dex appeared to have the wind knocked out of his sails.

Trey turned and began walking toward Earl's office.

Dex stood for a moment and then followed him in.

"Brothers, it is a blessing to see you two."

Deacon Berry sat in the room looking over the group.

Trey shook Earl's hand and looked over at Red.

"We are going to make a few alterations to this meeting. First, we will begin letting Deacon Berry attend. Sister Monique Jones also will attend to take notes. And as you can see, there are a couple cameramen in here."

Dex frowned and Trey wasn't really feeling happy about the situation either.

"This should be a short meeting, so let's get to it," Earl said.

"Now, the first thing we should discuss is a really sad thing and I hate to bring it up, but Reverend Dexter, it has come to our attention that Sister Dennis claims that you have been making passes at her."

"What? I don't believe it." Dex said angrily.

"You don't believe she came forward?"

"Shut off the camera," Dex said.

"The camera will roll. Now what do you have to say for yourself? Have you been making passes at Sister Dennis?"

"No."

"Well, we will have to get to the bottom of this. We cannot have a member of the pastoral staff engaging in behavior not befitting a minister."

"Oh, you don't want to go down this road. You really don't want to do this," Dex said.

"Or what?"

"I know for a fact that you have been screwing Carolyn Harold for the last—"

Trey angrily stood up. "You better shut up while you're still ahead."

"Everybody knows this. I know you ain't gonna get on me for this."

"None of this is relevant to the discussion. Did you or did you not make passes at the sister?"

"No, I did not."

"We have to take this seriously, so until we figure out the answer to the question, you are gonna have to sit down until—"

"Hell naw," Dex said.

"Well, what do you all think?"

"I think we should take all issues of sexual harassment seriously. I vote that we sit him down until we get this whole thing figured out," Trey said.

Dex looked at Red.

"We cannot let the church have any issues because of Dex's wrongdoings. However, we cannot fall into the trap of making the man guilty until proven innocent," Red said.

"How about we–" Terry said.

"I cannot believe what I am hearing, Deacon," Earl interrupted. "Sexual harassment is a serious issue and you want to let the man off the hook while the woman has to shrink away in shame?"

"Now come on, I didn't say that. I said—"

"Well, since no one wants to stand on principle, I will. I will set Dex down until this situation is totally resolved," Earl said.

"No one wants to stand on principle? Did you hear me saying the same thing?" Trey said.

"I heard you, and I am disappointed. The decision has been made."

Trey's face shrunk up. He then said, "Did I not say the same thing?"

"Well, if you said the same thing then why are you upset about the decision?" Earl said.

"Stop playing to these cameras," Trey said.

"I ain't playing to the cameras. I am making a decision. A decisive decision that needed to be made. And you are the only one fighting me over it."

"No, I'm fighting you over it," Dex said. "I haven't been with this woman and you are trying–"

"You should be aware that surveillance cameras throughout the church have caught various things and I can show a video. The same technology that got Trey's daddy got you."

"You know good and well that Dex and Red used faulty video on my dad," Trey said.

"Maybe we all ought to calm down," Terry Smith said.

"Yeah, you want to calm down now that we talking 'bout a video your fruity behind is in," Dex said.

"What's that supposed to mean?" Terry said in response.

"OK, everybody calm down. I see now that I'm gonna have to be the adult in the room." Earl said.

Red's nose flared. He said, "What the hell are you talking 'bout, Earl? You started this mess."

"Reverend Dexter, you are on administrative leave. If your name is cleared, then we will reinstate you," Earl yelled above everybody.

"Name cleared? I don't know anything about any court case. Nobody has told me anything. So you are setting me down on the basis of a rumor?"

"It is time for you to go. We have other ministerial work to talk about to those ministers in good standing," Earl said.

"So you setting me down 'cause of some mythical video, and yet you got a guy here who everybody knows got a boyfriend?" He pointed at Terry. "And another guy over there who has robbed the church blind?" He pointed at Red. "And you, you been having sex with Trey's sister as long as we all can remember."

"Get out of here!!" Earl yelled.

"The only person in here that got any kind of credibility is Trey."

"Do you want me to call security?"

"Security? When did we get security?" Red asked.

"The television show has some security."

"I'm going." Dex rushed out of the room.

Earl smiled. He said, "OK, now we can move on to the next order of business."

Trey, Red, and Terry looked at him skeptically.

"Now, I was planning to put you over on some youth work, but I think we should put you over the downtown mission, Reverend Harold."

"OK," Trey responded.

"But I have plans to turn it into a top notch facility, including Sunday morning services."

"So you are gonna get me out of the church?" Trey said.

"No, I'm gonna give you the opportunity to expand the church in a brand new direction."

Red laughed.

"Preacher, you are playing with fire," Trey said.

"And because we are losing two associates, I am going to name Terry Smith as a full associate, in addition to his role as minister of music."

Trey looked at Terry and asked, "So you in on this, too?"

"No, I didn't know a thing about it." Terry couldn't hide his happiness over the decision.

"Our final issue is the election for new pastor. That will be three months from Sunday."

"You emptied the church of all the other candidates and you made a new associate as one that no one would want to be the pastor, and now you announce the new vote. When did the placement committee meet?" Trey said.

Earl ignored the question.

"And there you go again defending Dex as well as attacking my desire to expand the ministry of the church downtown," Earl said.

Trey shook his head. He said, "These cameras here, they will be the downfall of the church."

Trey got up to walk out of the room. As he walked by, Shanese was walking in.

"Did I miss the meeting?" Shanese asked Trey.

"Yes, you missed the meeting, but I can see your fingerprints all over it," Trey said. He rushed past her out of the room.

CHAPTER 12

Shanese walked into the room and saw Red, Monique, and Terry.

"Ahh, here are the major players of the church," Shanese said.

"Well this major player is wondering why he has been left out the loop," Red said.

"You should be happy you're still sitting there," Earl said.

Red looked at him and said, "Ah, Earl, you getting a bit too big for your britches."

"That is Pastor Ellington."

"For real though, what's with making this guy assistant?" Red said, pointing at Terry.

"I sent a short video clip to the network. They love Terry. They love Earl. I don't know why, but they love you, too." Shanese said.

Red smiled.

"And for some reason they love Trey. The network wants a good versus evil plot. And because you are evil," she pointed to Red, "and you two are gray," she pointed at Earl and Terry, "we need a good one as some sort of offset."

"Did you get some good video of this meeting?" Shanese asked the fat cameraman.

"Oh yeah, wait till you get a load of this," the cameraman said as he laughed.

"Upload the video so we can get to editing it."

"We are almost done with the pilot. In your Sunday sermon you want to make sure to talk about the church vote three months from now. That will be the end of the season," Shanese said.

"So that's why you agreed to a vote three months from now?" Red asked Earl.

"It is time, it just so happens that God's timing coincides with the season finale," Earl said.

"Did you get Trey to agree to let his work in that mission be recorded?" Shanese asked Earl.

"He left before we could talk about it."

"That guy is a tough nut to crack, but we'll make do with whatever we have," Shanese said.

"And Terry, that date you were on was priceless," Shanese said.

Terry shifted in his seat nervously.

"Now folks, I have some work with the editing team to do. Have a good day," Shanese said. She then left the room.

Red started laughing.

"Looks like I created a monster that has eaten me," Red said.

"No one created me," Earl said.

"This whole reality show idea was mine. I shouldn't have done it. I shouldn't have fought Trey. Hell, I shouldn't have fought Carter," Red continued.

"Yeah, you shouldn't have lied on me in that video," Terry said.

Red and Earl looked at Terry like he was crazy.

"You just need to shut up and play the piano," Red said. Monique, Earl, and Red laughed.

"So Earl, is there any place for me in your new church?" Red asked.

"It depends on what the church wants," Earl said.

Red laughed and said, "I will take that as a no."

Terry said, "We all should wait to see what's in the television show pilot to see what's gonna happen."

Monique laughed and said, "I hope you get what's coming to you, Red."

Carolyn came to the door and knocked.

"Is your meeting over?" she asked.

"I think so. Would you all please let me and my fiancé have a few moments."

The group left. Monique gave Carolyn the side eye as she exited.

"Now what can I do for you, baby?" Earl asked. He kissed her.

She turned her head and winced slightly.

"Shanese said you wanted to see me."

"Yes, Sunday morning I want you to be with me as we have a special sermon and service. We need you to plan the election Sunday for three months from now."

"Why me?"

"Because you will soon be the first lady."

"We have a lot to talk about before that happens," Carolyn answered.

"And because a Harold needs to be heavily involved in the process so we can keep all things above board."

Carolyn said, "You mean so you can give the impression that everything is good even though it ain't. Who else is gonna be on this program? Can I name them?"

"Yes, but run them by my administrative assistant."

"Who is your administrative assistant?"

"Monique."

"Monique? Are you out of your mind? I can't even be in the same room with her. I told you not to hire her."

"Well, Shanese hired her. But..."Earl eased in and kissed Carolyn before saying, "give her a call. You don't have to be in the same room to call her."

"Oh, you get on my nerves," Carolyn said as she walked out of the room.

Earl sat back in the chair. It squeaked. Earl smiled All was coming together. He never would have thought a few months ago that he would now be getting ready to pastor a large church and be a television star as well.

The phone rang. He picked it up.

"Hello, we heard you are working on a pilot that is very close to being picked up by Lifeline Television."

"Yes."

"Well, we have some television time for your church that we would like to offer you."

"We can't afford it right now."

"Lifeline Television is willing to give you eight weeks free in anticipation of the television show launch."

"National television exposure for eight weeks for free? Has this been OKed by Shanese Jackson?"

"Understand, Shanese Jackson sells television shows to the network, but this is not through her or her show. We think the show is going to be big and we think you are going to be a star, so we want to get in the Reverend Earl Ellington business."

"What do you have in mind?" Earl said.

"First we will put your church on television. And if you get as big as we are anticipating, then maybe a talk show like Steve Harvey. Maybe a movie. The sky is really the limit."

Earl smiled and said, "Sounds good. What do I need to do?"

"How about we fly you and your fiancé to L.A. to discuss this?"

"Well, I preach Sunday."

"After you preach, get on the plane and let's show you the plan. It is good talking to you, Reverend."

Earl hung up and smiled. "They want to get in the Earl Ellington business."

CHAPTER 13

In the pastor's study sat Shanese, Red, and Earl that Sunday morning.

Red sat with a nonchalant vibe. Earl was pretty calm and Shanese was as she always is, determined and about business.

"As we have discussed, this is an important sermon. Do you remember what you are going to do?" Shanese asked Earl.

A devious grin cracked Earl's face. He said, "I preach the sermons. That's my job. I don't need your help on that."

Shanese stopped and said, "This is my show. Don't get it twisted. Don't mess up my show and make me set you down."

Red looked up at the two. He was obviously enjoying the fireworks between the two who seemed to have been closing him out as of late.

"Oh, is that so?" Earl responded.

"You starting to get on my nerves, Earl. You don't want to be on my nerves," Shanese said.

Earl smiled. "Naw, you misunderstand. I know this is your game, your show, but understand, you don't preach. I don't tell you which side to record me on and you don't tell me how to preach. How about that?"

Shanese continued to glare at Earl.

"In fact, now that I think about it, why don't you make sure you get me on my left side," Earl said as he pointed at his left cheek.

Shanese kept the same look on her face and said, "Yeah, you don't think you need me now."

"I need the Lord. It is better to trust in the LORD than to put confidence in man. Psalm–" Earl began to say.

"—118 and verse 8," Shanese interrupted.

"You know the Bible?" Earl said.

"Pride goeth before destruction, and a haughty spirit before a fall. Proverbs 16–" Shanese said.

"And verse 18," Earl interrupted.

Shanese laughed and said, "I know about you going behind my back to the network. You obviously are counting your chickens before they hatched."

"The network?" Red said, "What you got cookin', Earl?" Red continued.

"I didn't go to anybody, they came to me," Earl said, ignoring Red and answering Shanese.

"So you think you are gonna be a star without me?" Shanese said.

"That's what you told me," Earl answered.

"Well, I'm gonna let you know right now, if you mess with my show, I'm gonna take you down."

Earl laughed and said, "You forget the only reason why you are doing this show is because I am letting you."

"And you forget, the only reason Lifeline knows who you are is because of clips I sent them from my show," Shanese replied.

Earl stood up and grabbed his clergy robe and began putting it on. He said, "We are co-workers, and as long as we are co-workers, we are in this thing together. And now, I need to go into the church to address my congregation."

Shanese smiled and said, "We are co-workers as long as I don't mind working with you."

Earl walked out of the room with that characteristic smirk that was starting to become a habitual part of his face.

Shanese then said to Red, "We are gonna have to get rid of that guy."

Red laughed. "Oh, it's we now."

Shanese looked at Red and said, "It began as we, and it has always been we."

"You must think I'm stupid. You got rid of Dex. You got rid of Trey. And now you want to get rid of Earl."

"I'll get rid of you, too, if I have to," Shanese said.

"Let's get something straight now. This is my church. I brought you in. You don't want me as an enemy," Red said.

"You brought me in because you needed me for your little show."

Red stood up and said, "Whatever you say, Shanese, but remember, once you burn somebody, they will always know you are not to be trusted. Now I need to get into my church."

Red left.

Shanese continued sitting there in the pastor's study plotting her next move.

The sanctuary was full that Sunday morning, and Terry Smith had the choir in rare form.

They sang "There is a Balm in Gilead." The old spiritual was transformed by Terry into an upbeat powerful anthem of healing.

The song ministered to the congregation and even Terry himself took a turn at the mic by taking a solo.

The moment was not lost on Earl, who could see that even the most spiritual moments of the worship service were now becoming more and more times to grab the spotlight.

Terry, like many of the ministers and members, was playing to the cameras.

Terry used too many runs and his commentary went on a bit too long.

The announcements from the clerk were a little longer than normal. Every part of the service had people attempting to become a large part of the reality show.

After a lengthy service, Earl took to the pulpit, and he immediately grabbed the attention of the members.

He sat aside his apprehensions about the increased playing to the cameras and then took his turn at trying to put his best foot forward in their direction.

He preached a sermon about Namaan going into the Jordan seven times.

And the members were totally enraptured. Brother Bean made his trademark run around the sanctuary.

Earl opened the doors to the church after the sermon and ten people took their stand for the Lord that Sunday.

Sometimes the service felt like God was showing up. Other times the service felt like something else was happening.

But it ended well. As Terry led the choir in the closing song, Earl sat there thinking about how to end the service.

Shanese was glaring at him from her seat. He really didn't want to continue antagonizing her, at least not until he was well on his way to Hollywood.

As the service began to draw to a close, Earl stood up to make a few announcements.

"My sisters and brothers, just a couple of announcements: First, in consultation with our pastoral placement committee, we will have the vote for our new pastor three months from this Sunday."

"Amen," a few in the congregation said.

"And next, on Tuesday night, we will have a viewing of the reality show pilot that Sister Monique Jackson has worked so tirelessly on. You'll want to be here early to get your seat."

No one knew what to expect, but the congregation was very responsive to that.

"Yes, sir," someone yelled.

"Will you be there with me?" Earl said.

There was a large response from the congregation.

Earl then quoted scripture and walked to the back of the sanctuary to greet people as they left.

Terry followed behind.

As he bid the members farewell at the door, Earl couldn't wait to get on with his trip to L.A.

CHAPTER 14

Earl slowly walked to the airport terminal. He was early. When he arrived, he saw Carolyn seated there.

"I wondered if you were going to come. I didn't see you in church," he said to her.

"You didn't see me at church because I left quickly. And I shouldn't have come here," Carolyn answered.

Earl smiled and changed the subject. He said, "So how long have you been here?"

"I came over right after church. Nice sermon by the way," she said.

"Why are you so nice to me?"

"Naw, I'm still mad at you. I'm still mad at your game. I'm still mad at you trying to steal the church and then trying to turn my life into a television show."

Earl laughed and said, "Well, Shanese told me that she had to offer you a television show to get you here. But you don't believe her, do you?"

"Why shouldn't I?"

"She wants to use us. But Lifeline is being cool with me. And you are gonna really enjoy this trip. You and I are the real stars of this show and you and I need to be treated like it."

Carolyn looked at him and then picked up her cell phone and began typing with her thumb.

"You know I'm right. When are you going to get over yourself and work with me?"

"Work with you? You always playing games, Earl. I got a question for you."

"What?" Earl said with a little more spice than he thought he should have placed on it.

"Where is Monique? Why is that woman still around?"

"Shanese wants her. I didn't hire her. I can't fire her."

"Well, I don't like her around."

"I need somebody that knows the game. She knows the game."

"Mother Margarete knows the game."

"Mother Margarete is 87 years old. She *knew* the game." Earl said.

They looked at each other and then they both laughed.

Earl reached for her hand and said, "How about we just make the best of this trip?"

Over the speakers they heard, "Boarding for Flight 3008 nonstop service to LAX will begin shortly."

Carolyn turned her head and playfully said, "Whatever."

Beverly, Trey, and Lady Janet were in Trey's house eating Sunday dinner.

There was a knock on the door.

Trey asked who it was and before they knew it Red and Shanese were sitting in the dining room.

Red began chomping down on some macaroni and cheese and collard greens and said, "Lady Janet, one thing I have missed from your husband and I having issues was your collard greens. You really put your foot in this."

Lady Janet smiled and said, "It wasn't just my husband. You and I also had issues."

Trey then said, "And my wife and I."

"She ain't here, but Carolyn also had problems with you, Deacon," Lady Janet said.

"All water under the bridge," Red said.

"What do you two want?" Trey asked.

"Earl is not working in the best interests of the church," Red said.

"And neither are you. Neither is Shanese. So what is your point?" Trey answered.

"OK, I ain't gonna lie to you. Earl no longer has the best interests of the show at heart," Shanese said.

Trey shook his head and said, "And what do I care about that?"

"You don't, but you do care about the church, and if we work together we all can get what we want," Shanese said.

"Well, it was good having you two here, but I don't think we are going to be able to work together," Trey said.

"You want your church back. We can do that. We can showcase your downtown mission work," Shanese said.

"And what do I have to give up to you?"

"You just give us access. That's all I want," Shanese said.

"And I want to hold on to my position once you become pastor," Red said.

"I don't know if I can do that."

"If we don't hire you, we can hire Dex. You are interchangeable, man," Red said.

"Now hold on, Red and I are not permanent allies. We are temporary allies. If you give me access, that's all I want. AND once you become pastor, you continue to allow access," Shanese said.

"You are gonna crap on me again?" Red said.

"I have made my position clear. I don't want a television show in the church," Trey said.

"Now wait. This woman is going to help us get the church back and you can't just throw that away. All she is asking is to record you doing the good work that you are doing now," Lady Janet said.

"What do you think, hun? You ain't said anything," Trey asked Beverly.

"Well, I don't trust or like Shanese, and I suspect the feeling is mutual," Beverly said.

"No. Perhaps we just got off on the wrong foot," Shanese said.

"No, I know you, and you are a snake in the grass, but you are our only option right now. I say we take the deal," Beverly said.

"Great, let's get a camera crew over to that mission. We need to really play this up," Shanese.

"So you really think you are going to mess over me like this? I can call Earl right now and tell him what you are up to. His flight probably hasn't left."

"As much as I hate to say it, maybe we ought to think about working with Red," Lady Janet said.

Red smiled and said, "I knew you loved me."

"Ain't nobody said nothing about loving you."

"Trey, you need Red or this won't work," Beverly said.

This surprised Trey. He looked over at Red, who had a smug grin.

"We'll talk," Trey said to Red.

"Of course we will," Red said.

"How about this afternoon? Let's go ahead and get some footage of your work. We need to add it in if we are going to get it ready for the show's pilot," Shanese said.

"OK, OK, I said OK," Trey said.

"How about we bring in some cameras here? With you, the family and the good deacon eating together," Shanese said.

"I can't wait to praise your cooking on camera," Red said to Lady Janet.

Lady Janet rolled her eyes.

Shanese picked up her phone and said, "We need you inside."

She then walked over to the front door and opened it.

A couple of cameramen walked in.

"Oh, you knew what I was gonna say, huh?" Trey asked.

"I know what's important to you," Shanese said.

"And you used it?"

"Let's just take some pictures of the folks eating." Shanese said to a cameraman while ignoring Trey.

Trey wondered if he really should be making this deal.

Red did as he said he would. He praised the work of Trey in the downtown mission, which he had not seen. He praised Trey for his ministry. And he praised Beverly for standing by his side. He even praised Lady Janet for her cooking as he had promised.

The rest of the group sat around the table.

Shanese smiled off camera, for she now had every major player in the church on board and supportive of her television show.

CHAPTER 15

Earl and Carolyn walked onto the studio lot.

"Why do they want us at a studio?" Carolyn asked when a woman walked up to them.

Candy Bael, one of those actresses with a decent resume but who was now having a hard time finding work, walked up and greeted them.

"Reverend, hello, it is good to see you. I am glad you came out to meet for a discussion," Candy said to Earl.

"I am happy to be here," he said.

"The executives will meet with you later, but now, I wanted to talk to you. My name is—"

"—Candy Beal," Carolyn supplied.

"Yes, I wanted to talk to you about a show I am working on."

"You're working on a show?" Earl said.

"Yes, it is about an African American preacher who is seeking to help the people who are having issues in that community."

"That is your show? Sounds like my reality."

"Yes, I just love the African American church and your people," Candy said.

Earl frowned and said, "Your People?"

Carolyn laughed.

"Whenever I go to a church, it is an African American one," Candy said.

Earl said, "Me too."

"The network hasn't put a lot of money behind it, so the title role is open. I saw some of your clips from an upcoming show and wanted you to come in for it. Here is the script," she said.

Earl was looking at it when they were interrupted.

An overweight, pale, middle-aged white man and a fit elderly man walked up to them.

"Hello, my name is George Dance," the fat guy said. "I see you have met Candy," George said.

"Yes, she told me about this television show."

"Yeah, well, one of many," George said.

"Please excuse us," he said to Candy. He took the script out of Earl's hand and said to Candy, "So you are still trying to find a preacher for your show?"

Candy rolled her eyes.

George told Earl, "Clifton Davis already did that show with Sherman Hemsley twenty years ago, but we are in the twenty first century."

"Oh, it's gonna work," Candy said.

George turned to Earl. "Everybody got a script, but only a few have the money."

The elderly man said, "I would rather have the money than the script."

George said, "Go with the money."

George gave the script back to Candy and invited Carolyn and Earl into a golf cart.

The elderly man drove the golf cart around the studio. George pointed to various places where various projects were being shot.

They drove off road and then they moved on to another video set. It appeared to be a set with a church on it.

"OK, here is the deal. We have a movie. We think you are going to be a star, and our preacher has backed out."

"It isn't a big part, but we want to cast you as the preacher. Then when your reality show happens, it will make you that much bigger. And then you are off to the races."

"What is the show?" Earl asked.

"Ahh, it's a movie about demons attempting to take over a church and you are standing in the church."

Carolyn nudged Earl and said, "I don't feel good about this."

George looked at her and said, "I understand your apprehension, but we are talking about a healthy salary for a very small amount of work."

"What's the problem?" Earl asked Carolyn.

"Demons? What is this movie about? Do you even believe what they are doing?" Carolyn said.

Earl smiled and asked George, "So you have demons in this movie. Who wins in the end?"

George said, "Movies, they are just entertainment. I am not making any theological claims."

"So it sounds like you have a movie where evil triumphs over good and you want the good pastor here," Carolyn pointed at Earl, "to be the pastor. What happens to Earl, in this non-theological movie?"

"He dies when the cross comes off the wall and goes into his chest," George said.

Earl looked shocked for a moment and then regained his composure.

"Is this the message that a minister of the Gospel wants to send?" Carolyn asked Earl.

"Before you make any rash decisions, you should know that we have a few more shows in the works. If all goes well, the sky is the limit."

The elderly man who hadn't spoken much said, "If you want to be in this business, you don't get anywhere by turning down parts."

Earl nodded his head as if in agreement.

"Are you going along with this?" Carolyn said.

"Let's just hear them out, baby," Earl said.

The two men then took Earl and Carolyn back on the golf cart and took them to a room.

"Here is the deal. We have this part for you right now, and I think you will be happy with the compensation. Then, you do well in the first season of the reality show, and I am sure you have a lot more coming," George said.

"You think about it," the elderly gentleman said.

Carolyn was quiet for most of the walk back to the car, but when they got in the car, she began to let Earl have it.

"So you are now going to do a movie about demons and evil?"

"It's acting," Earl said.

"And what do you know about acting?"

"Come on. I know you aren't mad at me for wanting to take my ministry into movies. You trying to use this reality show to get your own show," Earl said.

Carolyn looked at Earl. "Yeah, I want a reality show. You keep bringing that up, but I ain't trying to make a movie about demons killing preachers."

"You ain't seen the script. You don't even know what's in it," Carolyn said. "And you ain't seen the script either," Carolyn mocked Earl.

"Well, I'm doing it. I don't even know why I brought you here. You don't even want to be a part of my life," Earl said.

"You brought me because your television show made us a couple," Carolyn said.

"And you went along with it because you want a show, too," Earl responded.

"You want to do the movie? Do the movie. I hope you get more than 30 pieces of silver."

Earl frowned and as continued driving to the airport to take the flight back home.

CHAPTER 16

The church was packed to capacity on the night of the viewing of the reality show.

Earl walked over to Shanese and said, "So how did it turn out? The first episode, I mean."

"It turned out good. I did make some final alterations to the show."

Earl frowned. And then asked, "What alterations?"

"You will see." She smiled and walked away.

Earl walked over to Red, who was standing talking to Trey. He said, "What up, y'all."

Red looked at him up and down and then walked away. Trey said, "What's going on?" in an uncharacteristically nonchalant way.

Earl started to feel scared, thinking something was up.

He then saw Dex smiling, talking to one of the women in the congregation.

Earl walked over to him and said, "How's it going, Reverend?"

Dex laughed and said, "You don't know, do you?"

"Don't know what?"

"Don't know that you 'bout to feel like what you made me feel."

"What are you talking about?"

"Oh, you gonna see."

The lights went out and Shanese walked up to the front of the church and said, "I am happy so many have come out to see this first episode of the show. Now, I have already showed it to the network and they have purchased two seasons, so we are off to the races."

"Amen."

"Yes, Lord."

And a few other affirmative words peppered the congregation.

"So here is the show, Broken Saints."

The show came on the large screen. On the screen, Dex faded in. He said, "I'm Reverend Dwayne Dexter. God is good, and so am I."

Then they cut to Earl and Carolyn. Earl said, "I am Pastor Earl Ellington. When God chooses you, you are chosen."

Then the screen faded into Terry Smith. He said, "Make a joyful noise unto the Lord."

Then they cut to Trey and Beverly: "My name is Reverend Carter Luther Harold III. I will always do what God says to do."

Then the screen cut to Lady Janet, who said, "Never, give up."

Then the screen showed a blending of all of them together with Lady Janet in the prominent space in the center.

Then the words "Broken Saints" blew up onto the screen.

The first scene was about Terry on a date with an attractive woman from the church. It was clear he was not fit for her. And they even showed him looking over at men.

This elicited a few nervous laughs from the congregation.

The next scene was Dex seated in a chair talking directly to the cameraman. Dex said, "Um, I didn't know he dated...I mean women...I mean..." They then cut away from him.

A few stifled laughs were in the congregation at that point. They were beginning to loosen up.

They then cut to a scene of Terry seated in a chair talking directly to the camera. Terry said on screen, "I liked her, but I don't think it was a love connection."

The next scene was Lois and Terry fighting over a solo. Terry took the solo and they cut to him singing it in church.

Then the scene showed Terry looking at the camera. "Lois needs to realize who the boss is," Terry said.

In the auditorium, Terry looked over at Lois, who stared at him angrily.

The congregational response was a bit lukewarm. They didn't really know what to make of Terry and his antics.

The next scene was of Dex. The screen captured him preaching and then flirting with a few women in the church.

It was clear he was a ladies man. The congregation again didn't really know how to take it.

After those scenes, the screen cut to Dex alone. He said, "I really wish I could be in the church more, but I have so many preaching opportunities that I must take."

Then the screen cut to Earl alone in a chair. He said, "I don't know why he gets around so much. Is he really a better preacher than I am?"

There were a few gasps in the congregation and Earl angrily looked at Shanese in the auditorium. She looked somewhere else.

Then the screen showed Earl scheming to get Dex and Trey out of the church.

Earl thought he had Shanese's assurances that it would not make it into the final cut.

On screen Earl was seated in Carter Harold's big chair while talking to Monique. Earl said, "Dex is unfit and Trey is unfit. I should be the pastor."

The next scene was from the minister's meeting where Earl sat down with Dex. The editing seemed to show that Earl jumped the gun to get rid of him.

Then they showed Dex alone, seated and looking at the screen gravely. He said, "Are they gonna get rid of everybody who someone has accused of something?"

The next scene was Trey doing a good job of preaching in the downtown mission. The screen then cut to Trey handing out food and playing ball with the people.

Then the screen showed Trey talking to the camera alone. Trey said, "I will go wherever they want me to go. I actually love this work and I love ministry, real ministry."

The next scene was of Red seated, talking to the camera. He said, "Trey is a very good pastor and I don't know why Earl is not making better use of him."

As Earl watched the show unfold, he got more and more angry. He couldn't believe what Shanese's editing was doing to him.

The next scene was the dinner where Red, Trey, Beverly, and Lady Janet were eating.

After watching a few minutes of them eating together, the editing showed a few one-on-one interviews.

"I really think the church should strongly consider Trey to be pastor," Red said alone to the camera.

"My son is perfectly suited," Lady Janet said alone.

They then cut to Trey, who again said, "I will do whatever God calls me to do."

Then they cut to Dex, who said, "I think the best thing for the church may be continuity. Earl is overstepping his bounds."

The final scene was of Terry singing, "There is a Balm in Gilead." The choir backed him up ably.

And the show ended.

"So what do you think about the show?" Shanese asked the congregation.

There was a halfhearted response.

Then she asked again.

There was a little better of a response, but it still was not great.

"Well, please go to the fellowship hall for some refreshments, and I hope you will continue to support the greatest new reality show on television."

She walked down.

And Earl rushed up, "What is this about?"

Shanese laughed. "It is about you thinking you are gonna go behind my back to do something with the network."

"So you gonna wreck the church?"

Shanese continued to laugh.

"Well, I'm gonna shut it down," Earl said. "No more cameras, no more nothing."

"If you do that, then I will be forced to make the show totally about Trey and his work in that mission."

Earl stopped and then said, "What can I do to fix this?"

"It's a long season. Maybe if you act like you got some sense, we can see what happens," Shanese said.

Dex then walked up. He said, "So how did you like the show?"

Red walked up and said, "So you thought you were gonna mess over me and get away with it?"

Earl then just walked away.

Earl walked to his pastor's study and called up his contact at the network.

"George, I just wanted to say that I wish to accept your offer and do the movie."

George said, "No, I don't think you are right for this part."

"What, a few days ago you were going to give me this job and now you are taking it back?"

"That's how Hollywood goes. I don't even know why I am talking to you now. I ain't got time to play with you. Let's see how the season plays out, but as for now, you're out."

Earl banged his hand on the table and cursed.

Earl picked up his cell phone and dialed Dex, who was seated in the fellowship hall talking to one of the women in the choir.

"Dex, OK, how bout you and I talk."

"So you want to talk now?"

"Let's talk about your reinstatement."

You could hear the smile through the phone. Dex said, "Cool."

Earl then called Red and said, "Deacon, I made a mistake. What can I do to fix it?"

"I don't think you can fix it, not with me at least."

"Give me a chance."

"I'll be listening."

Earl then hung up.

He then called Shanese and said, "OK, you made your point."

"And what point is that?"

"You are the HNIC," Earl said.

"You better believe it," Shanese said with a laugh.

"So what do I have to do to get back in your good graces?" Earl asked.

"Give me a good show, and everything else will be taken care of," she said.

"We need a meeting. You win," Earl said.

Shanese smiled and said, "OK, I'll let you know."

CHAPTER 17

The cameras were still in the pastor's study as Earl began the minister's meeting.

"Reverend Dexter, the woman has stated that it was not true. We are going to reinstate you as an associate at the church, effective immediately," Earl said.

Dex smiled. The chair squeaked as Earl slid it around.

"And Reverend Harold, I think we need to bring you back to the church. The work you have done is so effective, we need to get it back in the church," Earl continued.

Trey smiled.

"And the church will move on, with one major change. Brothers, let's make sure we put the business of the church first and no other concerns," Earl said as he looked into the camera.

"That's the only thing I ever wanted to do. Let's let God's work be done. That's the most important thing," Dex said into the camera.

It appeared that everybody was going to take a turn trying to look good to the camera.

"That's all I have ever said," Trey said as he looked at the camera and then looked away quickly as if he had done something wrong.

"This is a great meeting. I believe that God will be pleased in what we have done today. Red said.

"Amen, amen, and amen," Terry said.

Shanese looked on at the scene with a smile on her face. She was not on screen, but she was still a dominant fixture in the room.

Then Monique rushed into the room. "Pastor!"

"Yes," Dex, Trey, and Earl said at once.

"I mean Pastor Ellington."

"Yes," Earl said while looking at the other men.

"You have a visitor," she said.

Lady Janet then walked into the room.

"It is time for us to stop playing around and get down to business," she said.

"Lady Janet, you are not a minister in the church and you shouldn't be in here now," Earl said.

Lady Janet smiled and said, "I want to add an issue to discuss at the next business meeting."

"OK, but this may not be the best time," Earl said.

"We need to stop allowing the interim pastor to use his power to become pastor of the church."

Dex smiled. "Let her speak."

"And how are you gonna do that?" Earl asked.

"I am going to propose an amendment to the church bylaws that an interim pastor cannot become the immediate senior pastor of the church."

"No," Earl said.

"That sounds good to me," Trey said.

"So you are saying I can't become pastor if your suggestion is implemented?" Earl asked.

"Yes, well, unless you step down."

"And if I step down, who is going to become pastor of the church?"

Lady Janet looked around and then said, "I will."

Red laughed.

Terry's mouth dropped open.

"And the first thing I am going to do is officiate my husband's funeral. Not you." She pointed at Trey.

"Not you." She pointed at Earl.

Off screen Shanese smiled.

YOUR FREE BOOK IS WAITING

Follow Tommy Settles and the Gospel Singing Group Living Praise as they learn how God's grace and Divine direction can overcome any problem.

amazon kindle   nook   kobo   iBooks

★★★★★ "I love the story. The transformation of Tommy Settles was amazing..."

Sign up for the author's New Releases mailing list and get a free copy of the novella *I Call Your Name*.

Click here to get started: http://www.shermancox.com/freebook

DISCUSSION QUESTIONS

1) Should one simply allow God to choose you, or should one actively seek being a pastor?

2) What should you do if the senior pastor is actively undermining the ministry God has given to you?

3) How important is it to follow protocol in the church?

4) Should you actively try to remove a pastor who seems to be using the church to further his or her agenda?

5) Should a pastor be expected to be in his pulpit or in his congregation on most Sundays? How about Wednesday Bible study?

6) Would you leave Arise Community Worship Center if you knew all of this was going on?

7) Who should be pastor of the church?

8) Do you think Lady Janet would be a good interim pastor?

9) Do you think Trey should be pastor?

10) Does "waiting on the Lord" imply doing nothing?

11) How should the church handle allegations of immorality?

12) Was Earl right to set Dex down on the basis of the allegation?

Also by Sherman Cox

Bethel Community Church
The New Pastor

Broken Saints
Deep River
Balm in Gilead

Fundamentals Of Preaching Whitepapers
Four Waves Of Biblical Exegesis

CPSIA information can be obtained
at www.ICGtesting.com
Printed in the USA
LVHW110947031218
599064LV00001B/52/P